W9-CAG-807

☆ RISE ☆
Reading Is So Exciting!
A South Shore Day Services Program
Supported By:
the J.Jill compassion fund
AT THE BOSTON FOUNDATION

P2 Please return

The Toolbox

Anne & Harlow Rockwell

WALKER & COMPANY · NEW YORK

Copyright © 1971 by Anne Rockwell and Harlow Rockwell

All rights reserved. No part of this book may be reproduced or transmitted in any form or by any means, electronic or mechanical, including photocopying, recording, or by any information storage and retrieval system, without permission in writing from the Publisher.

Originally published in the United States of America in 1971 by Macmillan Publishing Company; published in the United States of America in 2004 by Walker Publishing Company, Inc.

Published simultaneously in Canada by Fitzhenry and Whiteside, Markham, Ontario L3R 4T8

For information about permission to reproduce selections from this book, write to Permissions, Walker & Company, 104 Fifth Avenue, New York, New York 10011

Library of Congress Cataloging-in-Publication Data

Rockwell, Anne F.
The toolbox / Anne & Harlow Rockwell.
    p. cm.
Summary: An easy-to-read description of the basic tools found in a toolbox.
ISBN 0-8027-8930-7
 [1. Tools—Pictorial works—Juvenile literature. 2. Tools.] I. Rockwell, Harlow. II. Title.

TJ1195.R633 2004
621.9—dc22
2003066562

The artist used watercolor on Bodleian White paper to create the illustrations for this book.

Visit Walker & Company's Web site at www.walkeryoungreaders.com

Printed in Hong Kong

10 9 8 7 6 5 4 3 2 1

For Oliver

In my cellar there is a toolbox.
It is dark brown where hands
have touched it.

It has a saw

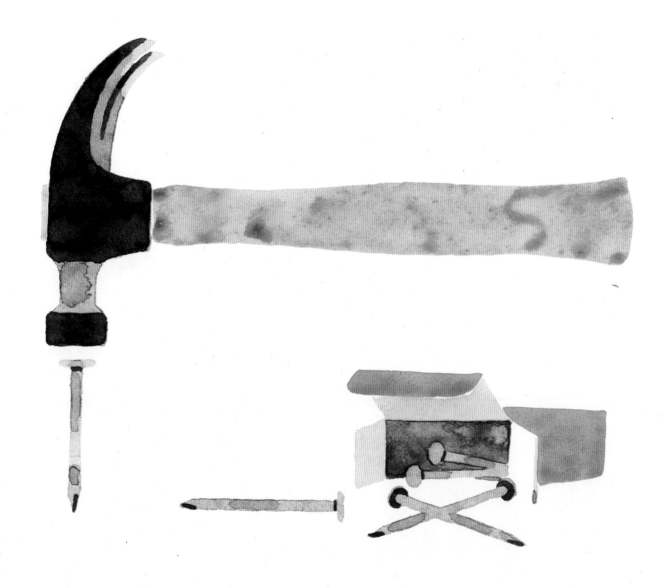

and a hammer and nails,

and a drill
that goes around and around

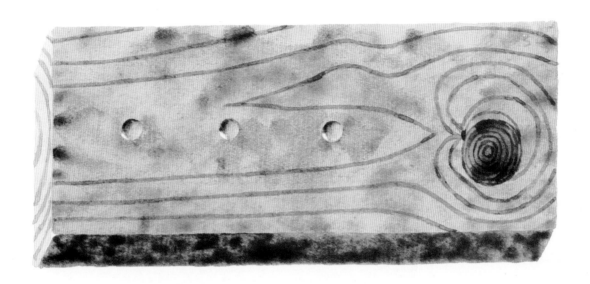

and makes holes in wood.

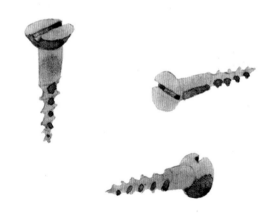

It has screws and a screwdriver,

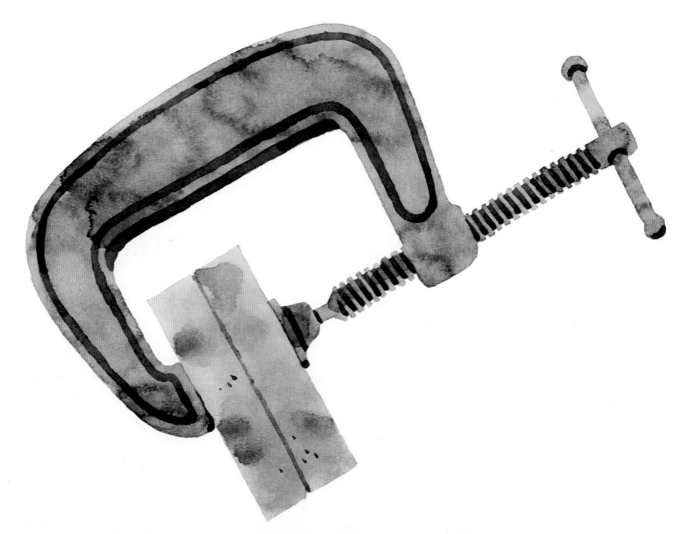

and there is a clamp that holds
pieces of wood together.

There is a big, strong wrench

that turns the big, fat nuts
and bolts,

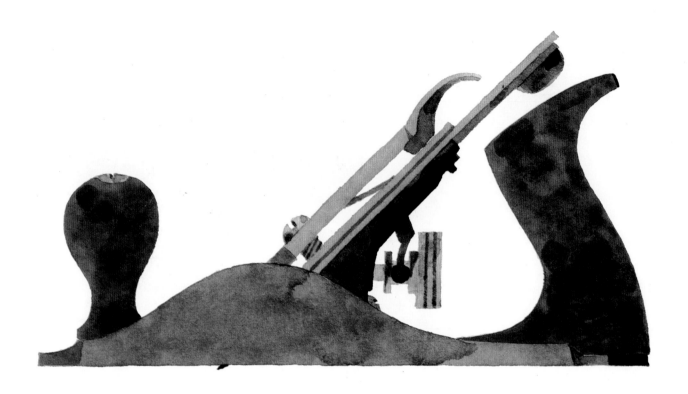

and there is a plane that
smooths wood

and makes curly shavings.

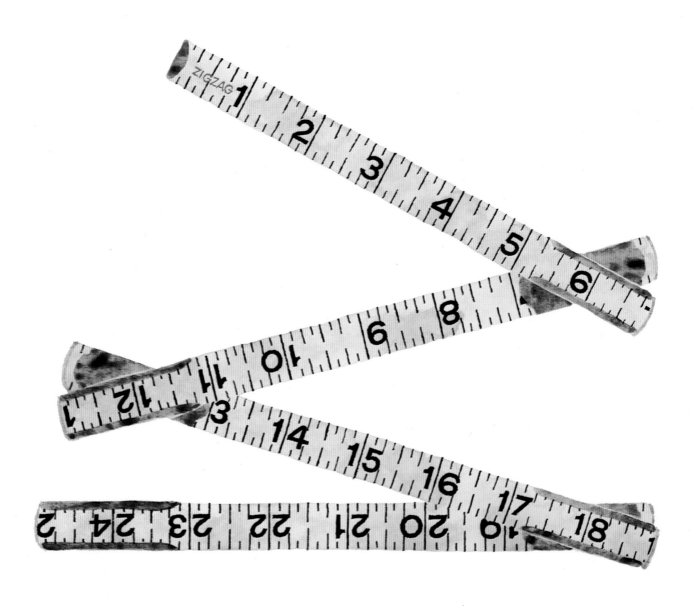

There is a ruler that measures.

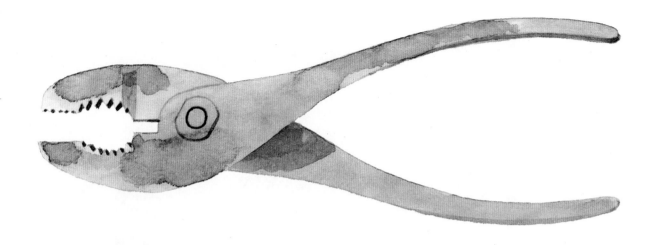

There are pliers that pinch.

There is sandpaper to smooth
wood and plaster.

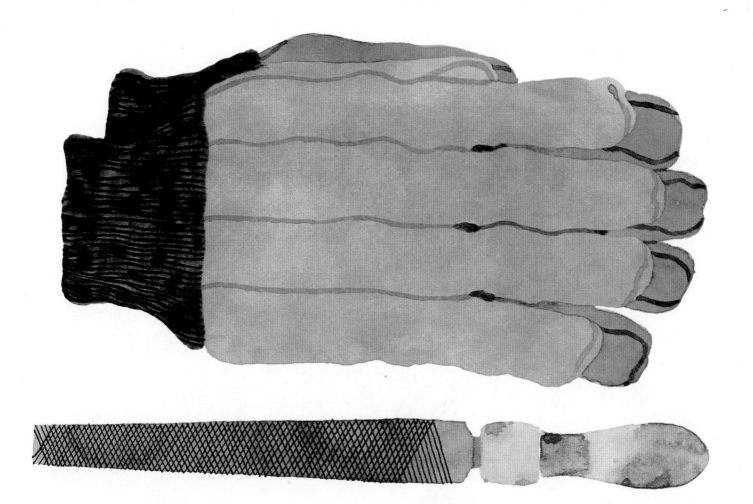

There are work gloves, and there
is a file to rub on rough edges
of metal to make them smooth.

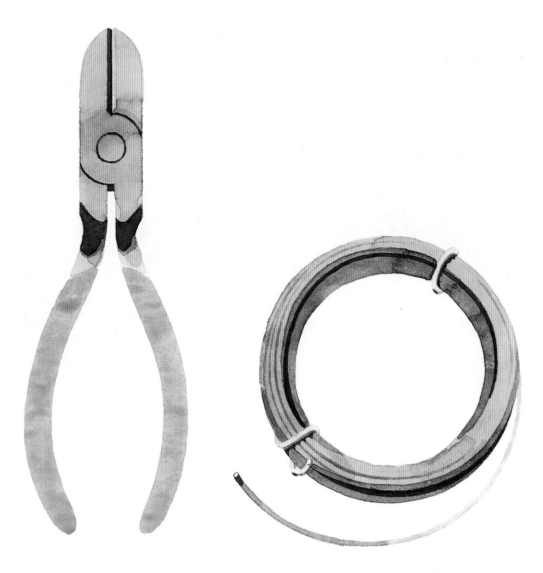

There are sharp wire cutters
and a roll of wire.

There is an oil can with
a tiny hole.

It is my father's toolbox.